DOCTOR · WHO

MICKEY

BBC CHILDREN'S BOOKS
Published by the Penguin Group
Penguin Books Ltd, 80 Strand, London, WC2R 0RL, England
Penguin Group (USA), Inc., 375 Hudson Street, New York, New York 10014, USA
Penguin Books (Australia) Ltd, 250 Camberwell Road, Camberwell, Victoria 3124, Australia.
(A division of Pearson Australia Group Pty Ltd)
Canada, India, New Zealand, South Africa.
Published by BBC Children's Books, 2006
Text and design © Children's Character Books, 2006
Images © BBC 2004
Written by Moray Laing. Taking Mickey by Justin Richards.
10 9 8 7 6 5 4 3 2 1
Printed in China.
ISBN-13: 978-1-40590-286-1
ISBN-10: 1-40590-286-8

CONTENTS

When Mickey Smith was a young boy, he discovered that things didn't always turn out how he'd like them to. His mum left when he was six, and his father went to Spain and never came back. Years later his adventurous girlfriend went off into time and space and left him behind too. So, luckily, Mickey learned how to adapt at an early age.

Mickey was brought up by his gran, a lovely woman called Rita-Anne, who he was extremely close to. He was devastated when she died after she had an accident at home.

On leaving school, Mickey became a car mechanic, at a garage not far from his flat. He started going out with a girl called Rose Tyler and the pair had an on-off relationship for five years. He always thought they were good together and had something special. All that changed, though, when Rose met a time traveller known as the Doctor. An upset Mickey watched as his girlfriend chose to go travelling with a complete stranger in a time machine disguised as a Police Box.

Over a year later, Mickey got the chance to travel with Rose and the Doctor in the TARDIS, and it was during his travels that he ended up in a parallel universe where his gran was still alive. Fed up of always being second best to the Doctor in Rose's affections, he decided to stay there. Somewhere where he could make a difference.

Name:	Mickey Smith
Date of birth:	22nd May 1984
Parents:	Pauline and Jackson Smith
Height:	1.65m (5'5")
Hair:	Black
Eyes:	Brown
Home planet:	Earth
Home address:	10 Bucknall House, Powell Estate, London SE15
Species:	Human
Profession:	Car mechanic turned adventurer

1.65m tall

Heart — broken several times by Rose...

Fit body — from working out and working hard as a mechanic

The TARDIS puts a telepathic field inside his brain so he can understand different languages

Contains his mobile phone, which he is always checking to see if Rose has called...

TEST YOUR
KNOWLEDGE

ROSE

One of the best things to happen to Mickey was meeting Rose Tyler. She lived in the same block of flats as him on the Powell Estate and he really fancied her. He was heartbroken when she chose to go off into time and space with the Doctor. But Mickey knew that Rose had to do what was best for her... and, unfortunately for Mickey, that meant travelling with the Doctor.

THE DOCTOR

The last of the Time Lords, a powerful race who were destroyed in the Time War against the Daleks. The Doctor didn't take to Mickey at first. He thought he was a coward, which, to be fair, he was! But Mickey didn't exactly like him either. After all, the Doctor stole his girlfriend. Before the Doctor regenerated, the Doctor liked to call him Mickey 'Ricky' to wind him up!

JACKIE TYLER

Rose's mum, Jackie, always got on well with Mickey. Until the Doctor took Rose away, that is. When Rose went missing for a year, Jackie blamed Mickey for her disappearance. She started up a hate campaign around the estate, which led to a miserable life for the innocent Mickey. When Jackie discovered the truth, that her daughter had become a time and space adventurer, Mickey and she became friends again. She would cook for him most Sundays and both of them would sit there wondering what Rose and the Doctor were up to, and if they'd ever come home…

PARENTS

Mickey's mum left when he was very young. His dad, Jackson Smith, worked in the key cutters in Clifton Parade, but Mickey was never very close to him. He never got the chance, as his dad disappeared off to Spain and never returned.

RITA-ANNE

With no parents around, Mickey's gran, Rita-Anne, became a big part of his life. He lived with her and loved her very much. Mickey was devastated when his gran, who was blind, tripped over at home and died as a result. When the TARDIS arrived in a parallel Earth, Mickey discovered that in this other world Rita-Anne was still alive. Upset but happy, he chose to stay there. A world where he could fit in and not feel alone.

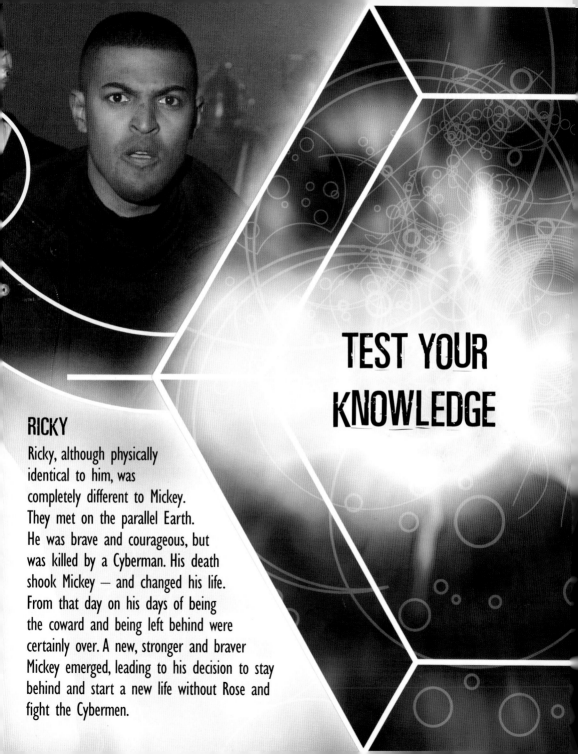

TEST YOUR
KNOWLEDGE

RICKY

Ricky, although physically identical to him, was completely different to Mickey. They met on the parallel Earth. He was brave and courageous, but was killed by a Cyberman. His death shook Mickey — and changed his life. From that day on his days of being the coward and being left behind were certainly over. A new, stronger and braver Mickey emerged, leading to his decision to stay behind and start a new life without Rose and fight the Cybermen.

LIVING PLASTIC

The Nestene Consciousness is able to bring anything made of plastic to life, as Mickey discovered when he opened a wheelie bin! The bin swallowed Mickey, kept him trapped underground, and made a plastic replica of him to trick Rose into telling them where the Doctor was. Later, a terrified Mickey was rescued by the Doctor and Rose in the TARDIS.

THE SLITHEEN

The Slitheen are a family of criminals from Raxacoricofallapatorious. Mickey first met one when it turned up in Jackie Tyler's flat and tried to kill her. They destroyed the alien by throwing vinegar over it and got covered in Slitheen slime as a result! Later that year he met one of the escaped Slitheen in Cardiff, but was more concerned about losing Rose than helping return Blon Fel Fotch Passamer-Day Slitheen to her home planet...

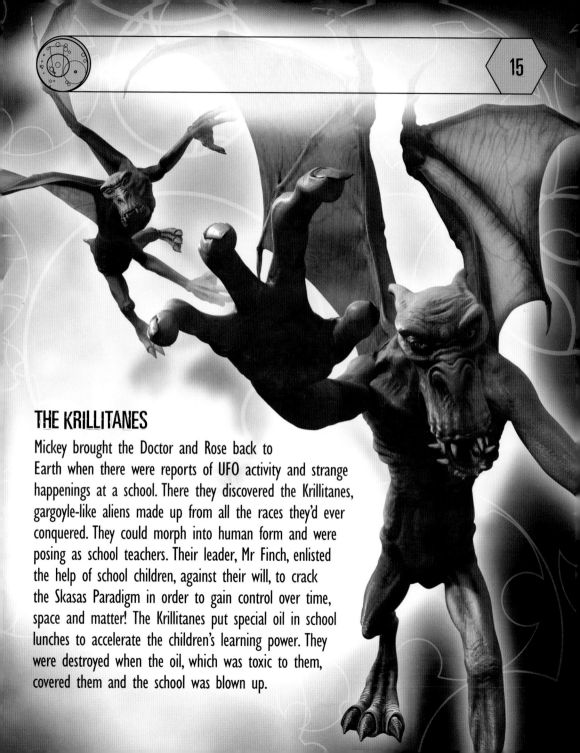

THE KRILLITANES

Mickey brought the Doctor and Rose back to
Earth when there were reports of UFO activity and strange
happenings at a school. There they discovered the Krillitanes,
gargoyle-like aliens made up from all the races they'd ever
conquered. They could morph into human form and were
posing as school teachers. Their leader, Mr Finch, enlisted
the help of school children, against their will, to crack
the Skasas Paradigm in order to gain control over time,
space and matter! The Krillitanes put special oil in school
lunches to accelerate the children's learning power. They
were destroyed when the oil, which was toxic to them,
covered them and the school was blown up.

THE CYBERMEN

On a parallel Earth, John Lumic, head of Cybus Industries, started 'upgrading' humans, turning them into metal monsters called Cybermen. Mickey helped destroy the Cybermen in the London factory and stayed on the parallel Earth to fight the Cybermen in other countries. When the Cybermen broke through into our world, Mickey, along with Jake and Pete, managed to come through too, if only for a short time...

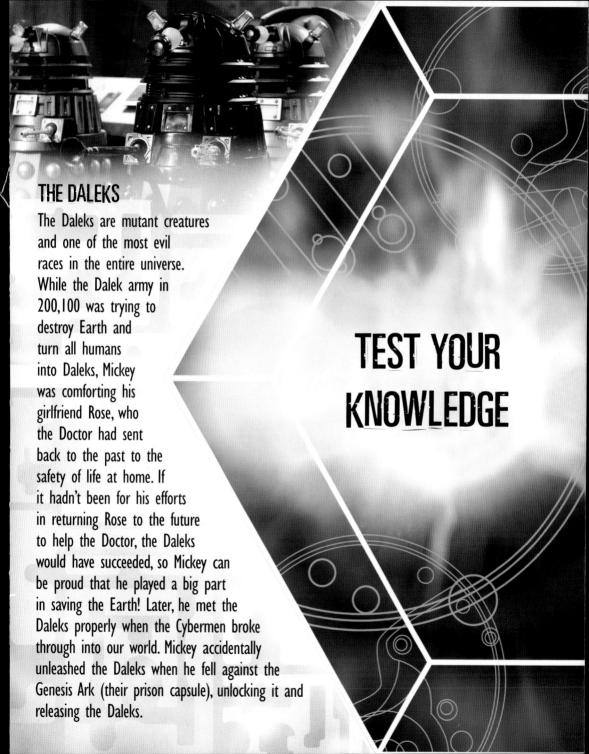

THE DALEKS

The Daleks are mutant creatures and one of the most evil races in the entire universe. While the Dalek army in 200,100 was trying to destroy Earth and turn all humans into Daleks, Mickey was comforting his girlfriend Rose, who the Doctor had sent back to the past to the safety of life at home. If it hadn't been for his efforts in returning Rose to the future to help the Doctor, the Daleks would have succeeded, so Mickey can be proud that he played a big part in saving the Earth! Later, he met the Daleks properly when the Cybermen broke through into our world. Mickey accidentally unleashed the Daleks when he fell against the Genesis Ark (their prison capsule), unlocking it and releasing the Daleks.

TEST YOUR

KNOWLEDGE

THE EARTH

Mickey's home planet is Earth. A generally friendly planet, the Earth is the third planet from the Sun in our solar system, positioned between Venus and Mars. It has one satellite — the Moon. It's not a young planet, it's over 4.5 billion years old!

The Earth travels around the sun at a speed of 108,000km per hour. As it orbits the Sun, the Earth rotates. This takes 24 hours (giving us day and night, day as it's facing the Sun and night when it's not). The Earth's journey around the sun takes a total of 364 days.

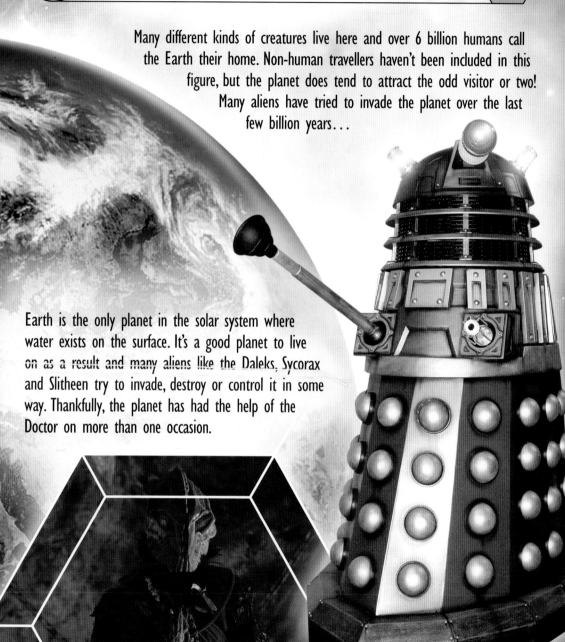

Many different kinds of creatures live here and over 6 billion humans call the Earth their home. Non-human travellers haven't been included in this figure, but the planet does tend to attract the odd visitor or two! Many aliens have tried to invade the planet over the last few billion years...

Earth is the only planet in the solar system where water exists on the surface. It's a good planet to live on as a result and many aliens like the Daleks, Sycorax and Slitheen try to invade, destroy or control it in some way. Thankfully, the planet has had the help of the Doctor on more than one occasion.

EARTH AND PARALLEL EARTH

Since Mickey met the Doctor, the Earth has been invaded by several aliens. Alongside Rose, he has played a big part in helping defeat them. He saved the Earth from the Slitheen using the computer in his bedroom; he helped Rose and the newly regenerated Doctor attack the mysterious 'pilot fish' who appeared ahead of the Sycorax; and finally, he played a huge part in ridding the world of the Cybermen and Daleks. Which was only fair, as he was accidentally responsible for bringing the Daleks back in the first place!

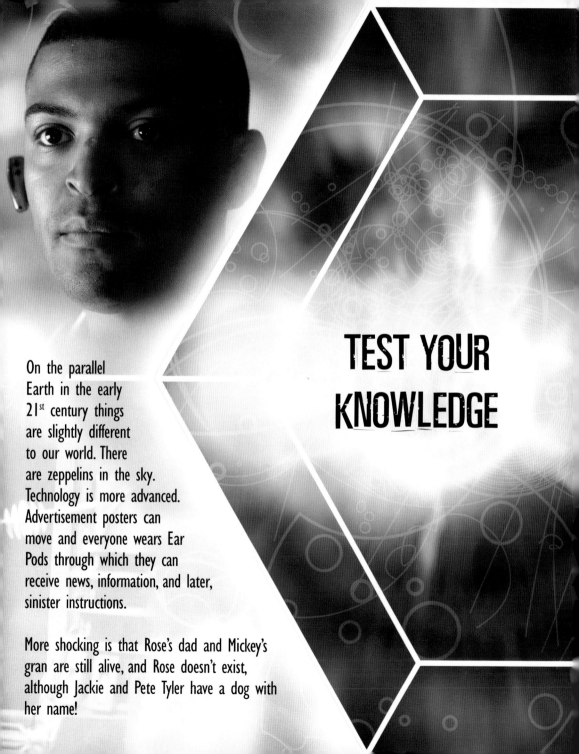

On the parallel
Earth in the early
21st century things
are slightly different
to our world. There
are zeppelins in the sky.
Technology is more advanced.
Advertisement posters can
move and everyone wears Ear
Pods through which they can
receive news, information, and later,
sinister instructions.

More shocking is that Rose's dad and Mickey's
gran are still alive, and Rose doesn't exist,
although Jackie and Pete Tyler have a dog with
her name!

TEST YOUR

KNOWLEDGE

BEETLE

Being a mechanic, Mickey is good with vehicles. He knows them inside out. His previous car was a yellow Volkswagen Beetle. He used it to take Rose to visit a man called Clive, who supposedly knew all about the Doctor. Mickey waited patiently in his car while Rose talked to Clive, but was lured out of it by a wheelie bin that swallowed him and then made a replica of him. When Rose returned to the car a 'plastic' Mickey drove off with her...!

MINI

Mickey used a Mini to try to open up the heart of the TARDIS. Mickey and Rose tied a chain to the TARDIS controls and tried to break it open with sheer force. The little car wasn't powerful enough though.

TRUCK

Mickey proudly claimed he once saved the world in a big yellow pick-up truck. When the Mini wasn't strong enough, Jackie found a truck and Mickey managed, eventually, to open up the heart of the TARDIS, which allowed Rose to get back to the Doctor.

ZEPPELIN

Mickey bravely took the controls of a zeppelin while helping battle against the Cybermen. He was able to rescue the Doctor, Rose and Pete with it and enjoyed flying it. When asked where he had learned to fly such a craft, he said it was all down to playing PlayStation games!

THE TARDIS

The TARDIS may be disguised as an old Earth police box, but it can travel anywhere in time and space, although it doesn't always arrive exactly where the Doctor planned. It took a while for Mickey to get used to the idea. His first trip in it was after being rescued by the Doctor and Rose, but he was too scared to appreciate the experience...

THE INTERNET

Mickey is a big fan of the Internet and has used it several times to help the Doctor and Rose. Initially, when Rose first left, he used it to try and find out about the Doctor. Later, he broke into a government database and helped to destroy the Slitheen; learnt about 'pilot fish' to prepare for the Sycorax attack; and wiped all traces of the Doctor from the Internet.

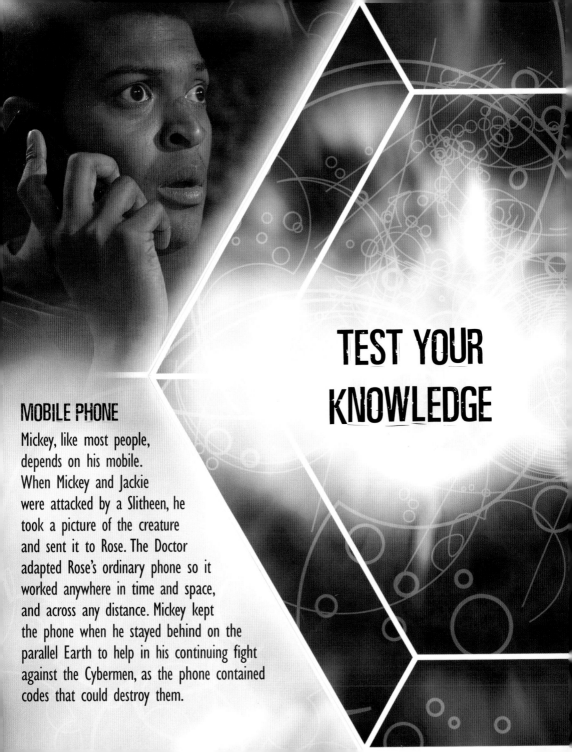

TEST YOUR KNOWLEDGE

MOBILE PHONE

Mickey, like most people, depends on his mobile. When Mickey and Jackie were attacked by a Slitheen, he took a picture of the creature and sent it to Rose. The Doctor adapted Rose's ordinary phone so it worked anywhere in time and space, and across any distance. Mickey kept the phone when he stayed behind on the parallel Earth to help in his continuing fight against the Cybermen, as the phone contained codes that could destroy them.

ROSE

After being eaten by a wheelie bin, Mickey was dumped in the underground lair of the Nestene Consciousness. He watched, helpless, scared and not believing what he saw, as Rose saved the Doctor and the Nestene was destroyed. It was all too much for him. While he was desperate to get away from the Doctor and get home to safety, Rose had other ideas. Mickey got a quick kiss, and Rose ran into the TARDIS and disappeared...

ALIENS OF LONDON/WORLD WAR THREE

Rose had been missing a year. During that time Mickey had been arrested and accused of her disappearance — even though he was completely innocent. He didn't tell anybody about the Doctor. Who would believe him? When Rose and the Doctor returned, Mickey helped them by launching a missile via his computer and destroying the Slitheen, but then they left him behind. The Doctor did ask him if he wanted to go with them but he thought that their dangerous life was too much for him. The Doctor gave Mickey a disc containing a virus that, when put online, would delete any mention of him from the Internet.

BOOM TOWN

Rose said she needed her passport, but it was really just an excuse to see Mickey again. He spent a day with the Doctor, Rose and Captain Jack, and they captured one of the Slitheen who'd escaped and was posing as the Mayor of Cardiff. Mickey was quite willing to trek all the way across to Wales to see Rose, but found himself bored of her constant talking about her travels. So he told her about Trisha, a girl he'd started seeing... and disappeared home to London, upset, without saying goodbye to the time travellers.

PARTING OF THE WAYS

Hearing the TARDIS land, Mickey couldn't help running towards the sound. He found a tearful Rose by the Police Box. The Doctor, to protect her, had sent her back through time, where he wanted her to stay safe and out of danger. When Rose thoughtlessly told Mickey that there was nothing left for her on Earth, however much he loved her, he knew he had to help her get back. So they eventually opened the heart of the TARDIS and off she went. Leaving Mickey behind for a fourth time.

THE CHRISTMAS INVASION

That Christmas Eve, while he was still at work, Mickey heard the sound of the TARDIS and once again rushed to see Rose. He and Jackie were almost squashed by the Police box, which contained a shaken Rose and a new Doctor. After fighting the Sycorax, the Doctor, Rose, Mickey and Jackie celebrated Christmas together. Mickey, along with Jackie, finally saw what Rose got from travelling with the Doctor.

SCHOOL REUNION

Mickey called Rose and the Doctor home to help investigate UFO activity and mysterious goings on at a school, which turned out to be the work of the Krillitanes. But someone else was also investigating, the Doctor's old friend Sarah Jane Smith and K-9, the robot dog that the Doctor had given her. Seeing Rose again and meeting Sarah Jane convinced Mickey that this time he wasn't going to be left behind. He asked if he could travel in the TARDIS and suddenly Mickey Smith was travelling in time and space!

THE AGE OF STEEL/THE RISE OF THE CYBERMEN

Mickey was quick to realise the TARDIS had brought the Doctor, Rose and him to a parallel time and place. He'd seen it in films, where everything looks the same but is really a little bit different. In this alternative world, he found one of the biggest differences was that his gran was still alive and that he had an alternative self called Ricky! Being braver and stronger than ever before, Mickey helped bring down the Cybermen and chose to stay in this world to destroy other Cyberfactories. Keeping Rose's phone, containing codes to stop the Cybermen, he said goodbye to his girlfriend and the Doctor, thinking he'd never see them again...

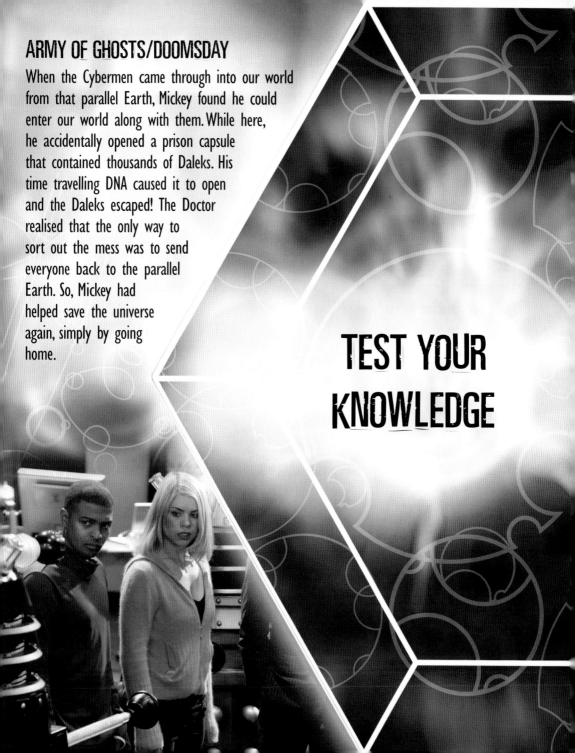

ARMY OF GHOSTS/DOOMSDAY

When the Cybermen came through into our world from that parallel Earth, Mickey found he could enter our world along with them. While here, he accidentally opened a prison capsule that contained thousands of Daleks. His time travelling DNA caused it to open and the Daleks escaped! The Doctor realised that the only way to sort out the mess was to send everyone back to the parallel Earth. So, Mickey had helped save the universe again, simply by going home.

TEST YOUR KNOWLEDGE

ANSWERS

Meet Mickey

1 (a) 2 (b) 3 (b) 4 (a) 5 (b)

Friends and Family

1 (b) 2 (b) 3 (c) 4 (c) 5 (b)

Enemies and Rivals

1 (c) 2 (c) 3 (a) 4 (b) 5 (b)

No Place Like Home

1 (a) 2 (b) 3 (b) 4 (c) 5 (b)

Transport and Technology

1 (c) 2 (a) 3 (c) 4 (c) 5 (a)

Adventures at Home

1 (c) 2 (b) 3 (b) 4 (a) 5 (b)

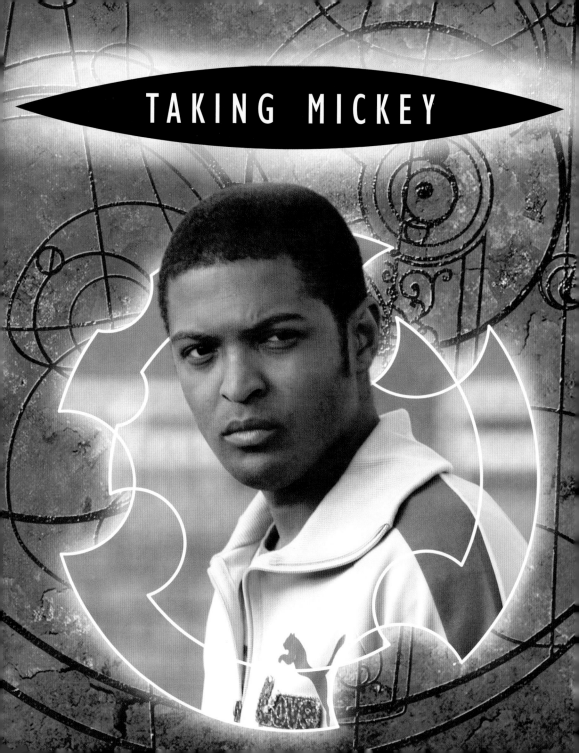

TAKING MICKEY

It was a Wednesday morning when Mickey got an email about the Doctor. He got lots of emails about all sorts of things because he had signed up to various websites about UFOs and aliens. It wasn't something he had set out to do, but he had sort of got into it. And it kept him busy when he wasn't down at the garage fixing cars. And it reminded him of Rose when she wasn't there.

He got lots of emails from all sorts of people. Mickey knew that most of what they said was just rubbish or stuff they had made up. But this email was from a woman called Jill Ongar who sounded very sensible. She said she wanted to meet Mickey because she could tell him things about UNIT and about the Doctor.

Mickey was interested in UNIT – a secret military organisation that knew more than they were telling about aliens and attempted invasions of Earth. He was also interested in meeting anyone who thought they knew more than he did about the Doctor. After all, Mickey knew the Doctor better than most people. Maybe Jill Ongar could tell Mickey

something about Rose too. So he rang the number in the email and he spoke to Jill.

She sounded very ordinary. She lived in London, not far away, and said she would love to meet Mickey. But he'd have to come to her house so she could be in when her children got back from school…

"Come for a cup of tea," she said. "I've got some custard creams."

Jill's house was on its own at the end of a row of very ordinary houses. But Jill's house was not the same as the others. It was taller and thinner, with a roof that sloped to a point, like the tower of a castle. Jill showed Mickey through to the front room.

"So what do you know about the Doctor?" Jill asked.

Mickey had hardly started his biscuit, and crumbs flew from his mouth as he tried to answer. He swallowed and tried again: "I thought you said you could tell me about the Doctor?"

Jill had told him a bit about UNIT, but nothing that Mickey didn't already know. It was all pretty basic stuff, really.

She held out the plate, offering Mickey another biscuit. "You can tell me," she said. "How did you meet him? Does he have any other friends? It's obvious from your emails that you know the Doctor quite well, though you try to hide that." She smiled, and Mickey couldn't help thinking that her teeth seemed very sharp. "Where do you suppose the Doctor is now?" Jill asked.

"I don't know," Mickey confessed. "Could be anywhere really. He comes and goes."

Jill was smiling again. "So you

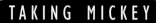

do know him." She clapped her hands together in delight, and Mickey couldn't help noticing how long her fingernails were. "And how do you keep in touch with the Doctor? When are you next meeting him?"

Mickey didn't like this. She was altogether too curious about the Doctor. He stood up. "I'd better be going. And you should be careful with all these questions," he warned. "It can be dangerous round the Doctor. Why are you interested all of a sudden anyway?"

Jill just smiled, baring her pointed teeth. They looked even longer and sharper now. "Do stay for another cup of tea."

"I don't think so," Mickey decided. "I've got to get back. And your kids'll be home soon anyway."

As he finished speaking, he heard the front door opening.

"That will be them now," Jill said. "Oh you'll like my boys. Such good lads, they are. And they do love to play. Perhaps you can stay and play with them?"

"I don't really play with kids," Mickey confessed. Actually he did like

playing football with children on the estate, but he was desperate now to get away. Something about Jill was making him really nervous, and not just the way she kept asking about the Doctor.

"Oh you'll like my boys," Jill said, getting to her feet. She seemed much taller than Mickey remembered. He was sure she had been about the same height as him when he arrived. Now she towered above him. "They're not like other children," she said.

And she was right. The small figures that came into the room were not at all what Mickey was expecting. They didn't walk in, they scuttled. They were about the size of small children, but that was the only similarity. They were grey, and looked like they had been carved from old stone. Tiny red eyes were set deep in their wrinkled faces, and their hands were claws. They reminded Mickey of stone gargoyles on old buildings. Except they were moving, they were alive, they were alien.

Mickey hardly heard Jill introducing them. "This is Yanta and that's Slopp," she said as the little creatures danced excitedly round Mickey.

"Er, yeah," Mickey said nervously. "Nice to meet you guys. But, hey…" He made a point of checking his watch. "It's getting late and I'd better be off. Thanks for the tea. And biscuits. Lovely." He was edging slowly across the room towards the door, backing away from Jill and her strange children.

"Oh no you don't," Jill said. Her voice was much deeper now,

rasping and angry.

"I'm guessing your name isn't really Jill," Mickey said.

"It's Jillonga. And you are not leaving until you tell me where I can find that murdering coward the Doctor."

"Tell her!" the two alien children said, in weird sing-song voices. "Tell her where he is, please."

"Then we can go home," one of them added, and they both nodded excitedly.

"Why do you want to know?" Mickey demanded, still edging towards the door.

"He killed daddy," one of the children replied.

"My husband," Jill said. She seemed to stretch up even higher. As Mickey watched she was turning into a huge alien creature that was a larger version of the children.

"The Doctor doesn't kill people," Mickey said. "Even ugly alien people," he added.

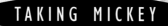
"My husband Bloodgrudge was a Trimestrian Warlord," Jill said proudly. "He lived for the hunt and the kill. He tracked the Doctor all across Wolanga without the Doctor even knowing. But when he set a boomer-trap, the Doctor just stepped over it."

"Yeah, sounds like him," Mickey admitted.

"Bloodgrudge ran after him, and the trap went off. The Doctor killed him!" Jill stretched out her huge clawed hands towards Mickey.

"Well, it sounds like he killed himself," Mickey said. "I mean, be fair. That's what happened really, isn't it? He sounds like a pretty rubbish monster, if you ask me."

Jill let out a loud roar of anger. "I tracked the Doctor here to Earth. I took my children out of school so they could see my revenge. Where is he?"

"I don't know," Mickey told her.

"Does that mean we can go home now, mummy?" one of the little creatures asked. "I'm bored. I hate my human suit and the other kids at school are so horrid."

"The food's awful," the other alien child said. "Can we go home, can we, please?"

Jill's gargoyle-like expression softened, although her face looked as though it was made of flaky stone. "Soon, darlings," she said. She stretched out her arms and gathered her children to her, pulling them

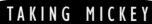

into a big family hug. "Just as soon as…" But when she looked across the room, Mickey was gone.

A grey, metal shutter slammed down over the front door. Similar shutters were covering the windows. The whole house was humming with power. Mickey realised that it was actually a spaceship, and he was trapped inside. He turned and ran quickly up the stairs, hoping to find somewhere to hide.

Something pulled at Mickey's jacket and he jumped. It was one of the gargoyle-children.

"Excuse me," it said, "but Mummy says we have to find you. Is it a game?"

Mickey nodded, his eyes wide as he tried to think what to do. "That's right. It's a game. Hide and seek. And you've found me. Well done." He led the alien into what looked like an ordinary bedroom. There were posters of pop stars on the walls.

"I like Earth music," the alien child said. "But otherwise it's really

rubbish here."

"Why don't you go home then, er – sorry, what's your name?"

"I'm Yanta. Mummy says we can't, not till we find the Doctor. It took us sixty years to get here. It would take another sixty to get home, so if we don't find him soon I'll be too old for school. Do I get to go and hide now?"

Mickey was about to say yes, when the other alien child, Slopp, scuttled into the room, its clawed feet clicking on the wooden floor. "Mummy's getting angry," it said. "She doesn't like you," it told Mickey.

"I guessed that," Mickey said. "So what's she going to do?"

"She says we can go home," Slopp said excitedly. The two aliens hugged each other and danced round the room. "She's going to keep questioning you on the way about where this Doctor is though," Slopp told Mickey.

"Oh, great."

"We're really going home?" Yanta asked.

"Mummy's set the controls. Once we take off we can't change course till we get home. We're really going."

"You mean I'll be stuck on this spaceship for sixty years?" Mickey said. "No way of turning back? Stuck here with your mummy?!"

"It's all right," Yanta told him. "We can play hide and seek."

"And noughts and crosses," Slopp added. "Though that's a bit boring."

"So why don't we play Airlock Runner?" Mickey said.

The two aliens looked at each other. Their little red eyes glinted with interest. "How do you play that?" Slopp asked.

"Well, we'll have to be quick. Someone goes outside the ship, before it, like, takes off, right?"

The aliens nodded. So far so good, Mickey thought.

"And the others wait inside the airlock door until whoever is outside knocks on it."

"Then what?"

"Then they have to open the door before the person outside can run away. Whoever catches him gets the next turn outside."

"But the ship's about to take off," Yanta said.

It was right, the humming was becoming a roar. Soon the ship would leave, with Mickey trapped on board. "So, we have to be quick."

Slopp was jumping up and down in excitement. "Tell you what, we could use the wardrobe instead."

"Oh," Mickey said, "er, no – can't do that. Because it's called Airlock

Runner not Wardrobe Runner."

The two aliens looked at each other. Then they looked back at Mickey. "Come on then," Slopp said.

"I'll go first," Mickey said. "So you can see how it's done, OK?"

With a deafening roar of its engines, the house took off and shot into the air. Bricks and cement fell away from the metal sides, and roof tiles slipped from the nose cone. Mickey shielded his eyes from the bright glare of the rockets. They wouldn't be back for 120 years at least, and by then he wouldn't be worried about Jill and her children any more.

Inside the spaceship, Jillonga left the main control cabin just off the kitchen and went to look for her children. They were sitting at the bottom of the stairs watching the main airlock.

"Did you find him?" Jillonga asked.

"Yes," said Yanta. "He's taught us a great new game."

"He'll be knocking on that door any minute," said Slopp. "Why are you looking at us like that, Mummy?"

The whole ship echoed with Jillonga's howl of rage.